What's My Word?

Chapter 1
HOPE

Summer vacation was nearly over and everything in Rachel's room announced the start of a new school year. Her school uniform was folded and lying on the corner of her bed, blazing white sneakers sat nearby on her bedroom floor, and a new backpack next to them — the perfect one for her final year at Rubye Irene Elementary School.

In just two days, Rachel would start fifth grade.

The *biggest* year.

The *best* year.

Or at least that's what she'd been telling herself to get over the nerves. Rachel always felt a little flutter of worry at the start of a new school year thinking about what her new teacher would be like. Only this year, the nerves were bigger than a flutter because she had a gigantic problem.

"Knock, knock," Rachel's mom said before opening her daughter's bedroom door. She took one look at Rachel sitting on top of the bed and then quickly turned her attention to Rachel's desk. "It's still here," her mom said, pointing.

"Like yesterday," Rachel said, and then sighed.

What's *Your* Word?

A message from *My Special Word* co-founder, Dwight Smith:

Our program, along with this book, wishes to remind us all of the power of words. When used with care words can empower a person like nothing else in the world. I hope that this story reminds you of the importance of words. I hope that it encourages you to help others find positive words that are heartfelt, warm, and inspiring.

Find your word!
-Dwight

My Special Word is a not-for-profit dedicated to sharing the power of words with children and teens. To find out more about the program or to apply for a grant to bring My Special Word to your club or school, visit www.myspecialword.com.

dedication

ded·i·ca·tion

noun

: a name and often a message in tribute to a person or cause
: devotion and loyalty

Addie, always take the tough shots. – DS

Greta, you've shown me what it means to
follow through. – AGM

What's My Word?
My Special Word Series: Book 1

Copyright © 2017 Alison Green Myers
Cover art © 2017 Greta Marie Schmidt
All rights reserved.
ISBN-13: 978-0692865187

HOPE

COOL

SMART

SURPRISE

TEAM

IMPORTANT

FRIEND

BASKETBALL

GOOD SPORT

WORD

What's My Word?

Alison Green Myers with Dwight Smith

"And the day before. And the day before that," her mom said as she crossed her arms over her chest.

The smile that spread across her mom's face let Rachel know her mom was just joking. They'd been having the same conversation since school let out in June. In August, just two days from fifth grade, the paper on Rachel's desk was as blank as it was the day she got it.

"Just giving you a five-minute warning for practice," Rachel's mom said before adding, "Why don't you just take a peek at the question one more time? I mean, you are my smart Rachel. It shouldn't be too hard for you to come up with one word." Her mom smiled again before stepping out of the doorway.

Maybe her mom was right. I mean, how hard could it be to come up with just one word?

Hard.

Very hard.

Very, *very* hard, Rachel thought. There are so many words in the world, how was Rachel supposed to pick just one?

On the last day of fourth grade, a guest came to talk to her class about a program called *My Special Word*. Mr. Smith, the man who invented the program, talked about finding a word he could *live by*. A word that helped guide him in the choices he made each day. When Mr. Smith spoke last June, Rachel's mind flooded with words. He was so passionate about his word and the *My Special Word* program that Rachel felt excited, too.

When Mr. Smith handed out the assignment, Rachel felt ready. Who cared that they were getting homework over the summer? Not Rachel. She would do everything that Mr. Smith had asked. She'd pick a word, *live by* it all summer long, and then write the essay that Mr. Smith wanted her to share at the beginning of the new school year.

But by the time Rachel left school that day she had heard so many other kids talking about their words, her heart felt like a deflated balloon. The other kids seemed to have taken all the perfect words. Rachel worried that she would never be able to pick a word that fit as well as the words her classmates found.

That feeling hung over Rachel all summer long. Every time she would see a classmate at the park or practice, she would pray that they wouldn't bring up *My Special Word*. Too bad, but they always did.

Rachel was sure that every kid entering fifth grade at Rubye Irene Elementary School wrote his or her essay and that she was the only one without a word. This was so unlike Rachel. She always did her assignments. She always took school seriously. But this time, Rachel felt like a failure.

In her room that August afternoon, just like all the days before, she didn't complete the assignment on her desk. Instead, she grabbed her basketball from the floor and left her bedroom.

Maybe basketball practice would take her mind off of the assignment? Maybe no one on the team would ask about her special word?

She could only hope.

Chapter 2

COOL

Rachel stood at the edge of the court, dribbling her basketball. To keep her secret, Rachel kept to herself during practice and games. Her teammates must've thought Rachel didn't like them anymore, or that she didn't want to be friends, but that wasn't true at all. Rachel wanted to be friends. She missed her friends. But she couldn't risk getting close and having them find out that she hadn't picked a special word yet.

Coach blew her whistle and Rachel jogged over to join the group.

"Hey, Queen Bees," Coach G called.

The girls all buzzed back. "Bzzzzzzzzz!"

Rachel loved being a Bumblebee Baller with Coach G. She loved being part of a hive, especially one with Coach G at the center. Practices and games with Coach G were the highlights of Rachel's summer.

"Well, bzzzzzzz right back at you," said Coach G, shaking her finger like a stinger towards the girls. "Last practice before the start of school. I'll miss my girls until the winter season starts in November."

No basketball practice till November? Rachel wondered if things could get any worse. But then Coach G opened her arms, inviting the girls to swarm her with a hug, and Rachel couldn't help but smile.

Coach G was the best. Her practices were challenging but always so much fun. And the games, well, Coach G made sure playing was fair and that the team worked together, all things that really mattered to Rachel; all things Rachel would miss until Winter League started.

After the group hug and some instructions from Coach, Rachel got busy on the free throw line. She sent ball after ball arching out of her hands towards the hoop.

"Nice finish," Nene said, joining her on the far end of the court.

"Thanks," Rachel said with her wrist still flicked towards the hoop.

"You okay?," Nene asked, retrieving the ball. She passed it back to Rachel before taking her turn on the free throw line.

Nene was Rachel's best friend, even though she hadn't seen much of her this summer. She'd spent time with her at basketball of course, but Rachel tried to keep her distance. She even skipped Nene's eleventh birthday party. That's right, she didn't even want her best friend to know she hadn't picked a special word.

"You seem mad," Nene added before sending her ball towards the hoop.

"I'm not," Rachel said. "Just have a lot on my mind."

"Tell me about it," Nene said. Her ponytail bobbed as she jogged towards Rachel. "But first, can I tell you a secret?"

Rachel nodded. It felt nice to have Nene sharing secrets with her again.

"I didn't do the homework yet for the *My Special Word* project." Nene looked around the basketball court. All the other girls were busy at different hoops with their own partners practicing free throws. No one heard, except for Rachel. And for Rachel, Nene's secret was the best news she'd heard all summer, or maybe ever.

"I didn't either," Rachel whispered back. "I'm so embarrassed."

"Me too!" Nene said.

"What are we going to do?" Rachel asked. "We have to read our essays at school in a few days."

"No big deal," Nene said. She sent another ball flying at the hoop.

"It's not?" Rachel asked. "Seems pretty big to me."

"I know my word. I just need to think of something this summer that I did to show it. Shouldn't be too hard with a word like *cool*." Nene made her thick eyebrows dance above her eyes.

"Cool?" Rachel asked, then laughed. "I guess you are pretty cool."

"I don't mean cool like super popular or something. I mean staying cool under pressure. Like during our game last week, when I had to make the last shot, or when the tire blew out on my bike on High Street and I had to walk all the way home to get help. Or…" Nene paused. Her eyes grew huge. "I know what to write." She did a little dance and rolled the basketball along her arms.

"Brutus ran away right before my birthday party. Everyone was freaking out but I kept my cool and went to all the usual spots he likes to hide. I finally found him under the neighbor's porch. Everything was back to normal by the time my party started. I kept my cool and everything worked out just fine."

Rachel looked down. She'd already felt terrible about missing the party and now that Nene brought it up she felt even worse.

But Nene's story did help Rachel feel better about one thing. Maybe she could think back over her summer like Nene did and find a word that she lived?

Nene had a head start. She already knew what word she wanted to use, but that was okay.

Rachel had always been good at coming up from behind. Like when the team was down by six points at the game against Dublin and she drained two three-pointers back to back. She could figure out a word and, just like Nene, get the essay written before school started.

Rachel took one last shot from the free throw line.

"Nothing but net," Nene cheered.

The ball soared through the air and sliced through the net. Cool!

Chapter 3

SMART

As soon as Rachel got home from practice, she went to her favorite thinking spot. Behind the townhouse where she and her mom lived was a great park. It was so close to her house that she could see her mom through the back window in the kitchen, making dinner. It always felt like she had the world's biggest backyard.

There were soccer fields, a Frisbee golf course, and even a walking path, but those places didn't feel like home to Rachel the way the basketball court did. Rachel dribbled to the free throw line, just like she had at practice with Nene and Coach G earlier. She sent ball after ball arching towards the net.

SWOOSH!

SWOOSH!

SWOOSH!

Then Rachel's mind wandered toward her special word. Just as the thought entered her mind, the ball sprang from her hand and tinged off the rim. Rachel went chasing after her ball.

"No follow through," her mom called from the kitchen window. "You've got to follow the ball with your hand. That's rule number one at the free throw line."

"I know. I know," Rachel said. By the time she caught up to her ball, her mom was out of the house and on her way to the court.

"Need me to come show you how it's done?" her mom asked as Rachel jogged back to the free throw line.

Rachel shook her head. She didn't need her mom to show her. Rachel knew just how to take the shot.

She kept her eyes on the hoop, stretched her arm out as she took the shot, and let her hand follow the ball to the net. The ball slipped through the net like butter on toast.

"Now that's some follow through," her mom cheered.

Rachel didn't say anything. Usually basketball could clear her mind and help her think. She could always count on shooting baskets before school to settle her nerves and get her heart pumping. By the time the bus would arrive on those mornings, Rachel felt like she could take on the world.

But that summer felt different. No matter how many shots she sank, a dark cloud of worry still hung over her.

"Everything okay, kid?" Rachel's mom asked, stepping closer.

"I'm fine," Rachel said quickly, but then she wondered if, like Nene, as soon as she shared her secret she might feel better. Maybe her mom could help. "Actually, no. I'm not fine," Rachel said. "I can't stop worrying about my word."

"Like I said before, you're my smart girl, so I know you'll figure it out." This time, when her mom said, "smart" she tapped Rachel on the head softly, then added, "Hint, hint."

Rachel smiled. She knew exactly what her mom was trying to tell her. "Smart."

Her mom nodded. "My smart Rachel."

Rachel tucked the ball under her arm. "Smart was the word I planned on using. As soon as Mr. Smith gave us the assignment I thought about the word *smart*. But when I was walking to the bus, I heard Matthew say that he was going to use *smart* and, well," Rachel paused and took a deep breath. "Well, I didn't think it was all that smart to use the same word as someone else."

"I see," her mom said.

"And then things got all crazy because it felt like by the time the bus pulled up on our street everyone had a word. Even the little kids were joining in with words to *live by* and Mr. Smith hadn't even visited their classrooms." Rachel smacked the top of the ball with her flat palm like a drum. "And you know the rest. The assignment collected dust on my desk all summer."

Her mom wrapped her arms around Rachel. "You're still my smart girl," she said, squeezing her into a hug. "You'll figure it out."

Rachel relaxed into the warmth of her mom's arms. The hug felt like a sprinkle of magic.

Suddenly figuring out her word didn't feel so tough. She would stick to her plan.

Find a word.

Think about her summer.

Write an essay.

Like Nene said. Just like sinking a basketball into a hoop, she'd do it step by step by step. Her mom was right; she was smart!

Chapter 4

SURPRISE

"Knock, knock." Rachel's mom's voice came through Rachel's closed door early the next morning.

"What time is it?" Rachel asked, rubbing the sleep from her eyes and sitting up.

She watched as her mom walked across her small bedroom, turning on lights. She clicked the lamp near Rachel's head, then the one on the desk, and finally pulled the string to click on the light in Rachel's closet.

"What are you doing?" Rachel asked, groggily. "What time is it?" she repeated.

"Time for you to get your bones out of bed and get dressed. There's a surprise waiting for you downstairs." Rachel's mom spun around in front of her daughter's closet. "I'd say this shirt." She tossed one of Rachel's Bumblebee Baller shirts across the room. "And these shorts."

Rachel tilted her head, still trying to process her mom's words. A surprise?

"Or wear whatever you want, but get your teeth brushed and your buns downstairs before they leave without you," her mom said as she danced towards the bedroom door.

Rachel slipped past her mom, ran out of her room, and slowed to a stop at the top of the staircase. At the bottom of the steps she saw Coach G's winning smile.

"I'm not taking you to Cedar Point in your jammies," Coach G called up the stairs.

Nene popped into view next. She ran up the stairs, two at a time, and collided into her best friend. "Isn't this awesome? Coach got one of those long vans. She picked me up first. We've been surprising the team all morning. Everyone's here."

"Time's ticking," Coach G said. "On the road in five minutes so we can get in line before there is a line."

Cedar Point was one of Rachel's favorite places on earth. The rides there were awesome. Rachel thought that she'd missed her chance to go to Cedar Point since school started in one day. But Coach showed up and surprised them all with a trip, just when Rachel needed it most.

Rachel and Nene zoomed into Rachel's bedroom. Nene grabbed sneakers and socks while Rachel tugged on her t-shirt and shorts.

"I'll brush and be right down," Rachel said.

Nene touched Rachel's desk on her way out of the bedroom. "I wrote mine last night. Guess you'll have to wait until our adventure with Coach is over to get your essay written."

Nene headed for the stairs, but Rachel stood frozen for a minute at her desk. She nearly forgot about the essay in all her excitement. She only had one day left to do it but she couldn't miss the trip with Coach G and the team.

"Rachel," a voice called from the bottom of the stairs. "We'll be in the van."

Her mom appeared at Rachel's doorway again. "Honey, they're leaving." She pointed down the hallway towards the bathroom. "Teeth. Now."

"But…" Rachel began. She tapped her finger on the assignment.

"Today could be the adventure you write about in your essay," her mom said. "You won't know unless you go!"

Rachel took one last look at Mr. Smith's homework page.

It read, *"Choose a word to live by all summer long. Tell me about a time your word helped guide you over the summer."* She drew a deep breath.

"That assignment will still be here when you get home, but the van might not wait," her mom said. "I guess I should've told you about the trip. I could've made you do the assignment last night. But when Coach G asked the parents for permission, she really wanted to keep it a surprise. I'm sorry I didn't tell you." Her mom bit her lip like she did when she was worried.

"Thanks for keeping it a surprise. It's great. I'll do this when I get home," Rachel said. She couldn't stand to see her mom look so upset.

"That's my Smart Girl," her mom said. "I packed a bag for you with a few bucks, your water bottle, and a Z-Bar. It's downstairs."

"Thanks, Mom," Rachel said. "For everything."

Rachel followed her mom out of the room. She gave her teeth a quick brush and took a millisecond to splash cold water on her face. She felt jazzed again, ready to ride all of those Cedar Point roller coasters. Like her mom said, maybe her story was waiting for her at the amusement park. That would be an even greater surprise!

Chapter 5

TEAM

Caitlin's mom sat in the passenger seat of the van. Rachel's teammates squeezed side-by-side in the back. It wasn't until Nene yelled, "I've got your spot over here" and tapped the small space beside her, that Rachel believed there was a place for her to fit.

Rachel climbed in and shimmied into a spot at the very back of the van.

"Hey, busy bees, everyone buckled?" Coach G called from the driver's seat.

A loud buzz replied back to Coach. The sound was louder than any noise they'd made at practice all summer long. The girls were beyond excited for the big trip to Cedar Point.

Rachel sang along with the girls as Coach G filled the van with her favorite playlist. The two hours it took to get to the amusement park went by in a flash.

"Bring your bags and your smiles," Coach G said before hopping out of the van. She jogged around to the double doors on the side of the van to let the team out. But once she got there, Coach G stood at the side for a minute, facing the girls inside.

The girls laughed at first as Coach G stared at them. Rachel felt like a fish at the aquarium with Coach watching them the way she was. The other girls grew quiet too. Coach's lips went from a grin to a serious line. When Coach G opened the doors, the van was pin-drop silent. Rachel squirmed a bit in her seat waiting for Coach to say something to break the silence.

"Your parents trusted me to bring you here today to celebrate our great season," Coach G started. She paused looking from girl to girl. "And they expect that I will bring you all home in one piece. You know what I mean?"

The whole van shook as the girls nodded their understanding. A few girls said, "Yes, Coach."

"We stick tight inside the park because we are a team. Bumblebees swarm the coasters together. If you need something, you ask me or Caitlin's mom." She pointed to Mrs. Benson. "Don't just wander off. Okay?"

"Yes! Coach!" they all shouted.

Coach stepped back from the doors and the girls sprang out of the van. They gathered in a circle, just like they would before games. Coach put her hand in the center and each girl placed a hand in, too.

"Buzz on three," Coach G said. "One, two, three."

"Bzzzzzzzzzzzz." The sound filled the parking lot and people turned to look at the swarm of Coach G's bees.

"We better get in there before all those lookers beat us to the coasters," Coach G said, excited. The girls followed Coach and Mrs. Benson to the ticket booth where each girl got a wristband and park map.

When Rachel stepped through the ticket area and saw the big carousel facing her, a knowing smile spread across her face. This was just what she needed to take her mind off Mr. Smith's assignment.

Her teammates hadn't talked about their words on the ride to the park at all, and now that they were around all of the rides, Rachel was almost certain that *My Special Word* would be the farthest thing from anyone's mind.

She was sure that a day at Cedar Point with her team would keep the pressure of finding a word off her mind, too.

That was until Caitlin put her hands on her hips and said, "Well, my special word is B-R-A-V-E so point me to the nearest roller coaster."

Everyone cracked up, except for Rachel.

"The Raptor is the closest coaster," Coach G said. "Not everyone is tall enough to ride that one. Let's go over to the Iron Dragon instead."

The girls took off towards the ride but Rachel hung back. As soon as Coach G noticed Rachel, she stopped and waited. When Rachel got to Coach G's side, she couldn't look at her. She was afraid if she saw Coach's eyes she might burst into tears.

"What's up, Rachel?" Coach asked. "It's been a rough season for you, hasn't it?"

Rachel sighed. Even though she tried to hide it at practice, Coach noticed her bad mood this season. "I never brought it on the court," Rachel said, hoping Coach noticed that, too.

"I know. You have the greatest follow through of anyone on our team. When times get tough, I know you're going to step up. When we need points, you're my girl." Coach put her arm around Rachel's shoulders. "That's not what's got you bummed today. Hate roller coasters or something?"

"No," Rachel said. "I love them. Today is great, Coach. Seriously, thank you." Rachel wanted to be sure that Coach knew how special a team trip like this was to her.

"Then?" Coach asked.

Rachel looked ahead at the team, all of them walking arm in arm through the park. She wanted to be up there with them but she couldn't shake the feeling that she was letting everybody down.

"You know how everyone has been talking about *My Special Word* at practice this summer?" Rachel asked.

Coach nodded. "Sure. Nene is *cool*. Caitlin is *brave*. Michelle is a *fighter*." She pointed to the girls ahead as she said the words. "I think it's awesome."

Rachel looked down at her hands. Her shoulders sank even lower.

"You don't have a word, do you?" Coach asked.

Rachel shook her head. "I loved Mr. Smith's presentation. He was so great. He talked about picking a word to *live by*. A word that made you feel powerful. A word that made you feel confident. A word that made you feel like you could make the world a better place. Who wouldn't want a word like that?"

"Wow. That does sound amazing," Coach agreed.

Rachel saw Coach's forehead scrunch up the way it did when she was thinking up a new defense or getting ready to call a play. "Even you know your word, don't you, Coach?" She finally asked.

"It just popped into my head," Coach said. "*Team*. I love succeeding as a group, whether it's with you girls on the court or with my co-workers. I know that alone I can be good but together, with everyone else's support and strengths, we can be great."

"That's a perfect word for you, Coach," Rachel said with a hint of a smile.

"We'll find your word today, too," Coach said. "We'll have the team help. Your teammates know you. One brain alone is good but all of our brainpower together, well, that's great."

There was just one problem. "Then everyone will know I dropped the ball on the assignment," she said.

"Better to let everyone know and get help than to have the weight of it resting all on your shoulders. We are a team. A good team always supports its players."

Rachel felt something swell inside her chest. She looked at the team in front of her. They did know her and, just like when Nene shared her secret at practice the day before; it felt better to know someone else shared her problem. Maybe the team could help?

"Here's the plan," Coach said. "Let's tackle the roller coasters while we're at the park and tackle your word on the ride home."

"Okay, Coach," Rachel agreed.

Just then Nene turned around and called to Coach and Rachel. "Hurry up! We want to all get on the ride together, as a team."

Coach smiled at Rachel. Rachel smiled back. They jogged up to join the team. Her friends pulled her into the center of the pack. There was a ton of laughing and Rachel felt really happy.

Coach was right. It was great to be part of a team.

Chapter 6

IMPORTANT

The day at Cedar Point was perfect. Not only

did no one throw up from The Corkscrew's

whips and turns but, more importantly for

Rachel, the whole team understood when she

shared her problem on the ride home.

They gave her lots of words to think about. *Smart* was definitely the most popular. Rachel's heart grew warm hearing her teammates describe her with words like: *leader, kind, thoughtful, caring,* and *friend.*

The van pulled up to Rachel's house and Coach got out to walk Rachel to the door.

"I think you'll nail this essay," Coach said as they reached the doorstep.

"Thanks for your help, Coach."

Rachel's mom opened the door. "How was it?" she asked.

"Great!" Rachel said, and she meant it.

Coach hesitated on the step. "I've got to know, Rachel. What word did you pick?" she asked.

But Rachel hadn't quite decided. "Not sure."

"At least tell me if we helped," Coach said.

"Definitely," Rachel said.

"Sounds like we've got a little homework to do. Thanks for reminding us, Coach," Rachel's mom said.

"Thanks for everything, Coach," Rachel said before closing the door.

Back inside, Rachel told her mom all about the trip: how they went on the Millennium Force three times in a row, how they ate at Johnny Rockets and how the waitress got up on the table to sing "Yakety Yak" to the team, and finally, how the girls gave her suggestions for words on the ride home.

"Which one did you pick?" Her mom asked excitedly.

"I didn't. The words were great. Really nice. But they weren't *my* word," Rachel said. She didn't seem sad though, just the opposite. For the first time all summer, when Rachel talked about finding her word, she was confident.

This puzzled Rachel's mom. "You still don't have a word?"

"Nope. And I think that's okay." Rachel grabbed her bag from the table and started up the stairs.

"Hold on, hold on," her mom called after her. "You don't have a word and your assignment is due tomorrow?"

Rachel nodded.

"And you're happy about this? Not worried and sad like you've been all summer?"

Rachel just smiled.

"Honey," her mom said. "I don't get it."

"Mr. Smith doesn't just want us to come up with a word for this assignment," Rachel said.

"He *doesn't?*" her mom asked.

"Nope. He wants us to find a word to *live by*. I'm just going to tell my teacher that this is too important a decision to rush. I'll tell him that I'm working on it. I'll tell him I need more time. I'll tell him that I'm ready to face the consequences of not having an essay if it means figuring out my special word to *live by*."

Rachel's mom was speechless for a moment. "If that's what you want to do, *and* as long as you are really ready to face the consequences, then I support your decision."

"I'm going to lay out my uniform and get my backpack ready for tomorrow," Rachel said, continuing up the steps.

"Okay. I'll be up in a bit to read with you," her mom said.

Rachel turned around for one last look. Her mom bit her lip and Rachel knew this meant that she wanted to say something else. Rachel thought that she probably wanted to tell her to just DO THE HOMEWORK, but somehow her mom kept that inside. Rachel was glad.

This was the first time all summer that finding a word felt like it did when she first heard Mr. Smith talk about *My Special Word*.

Rachel was determined to do it right, which might involve some explaining. Going one-to-one with her new teacher might be a challenge, but to Rachel, it would be worth it. Finding the right word was important.

Chapter 7

FRIEND

Rachel took her positive attitude with her the

next day. She got to her new classroom before

the teacher had even arrived. She found a hook,

hung up her backpack, and wandered around

the room until she found the desk with her

name on top.

Rachel smiled, noticing that Nene's desk was right in front of her. Caitlin was nearby, too.

"Good morning. You must be my early bird," a tall man said, walking into the room. "I'm Mr. Massey," he stretched his hand toward Rachel. "Maybe you've seen me around the halls?"

"Good morning," Rachel said. She took a deep breath like she would at the free throw line. She focused on Mr. Massey's kind face. "I came early this morning because I have something important to tell you."

"Oh? I'm all ears," he said, placing a stack of papers on his desk.

But now that Rachel was standing face-to-face with her new teacher, she'd forgotten the speech she practiced on the ride to school with her mom. In this classroom, on the first day of fifth grade, she was having trouble making any words come out of her mouth.

Mr. Massey straightened the papers on his desk. "We'll have company in a minute or two. A brand new student and his parents are coming for an early visit. If you have something important to say, let's hear it."

Rachel hesitated. She watched as Mr. Massey peeked at his watch. Time was ticking away.

Rachel knew it would be a busy morning for him but she wanted to tell him the truth about the essay before it came time to read them in class. She wanted him to know how seriously she took the assignment and how much she cared about finding the right word.

She cleared her throat and started again. "I didn't do the homework," Rachel blurted out.

Mr. Massey pursed his lips but didn't speak.

"I think that Mr. Smith gave a terrific talk last year," Rachel said.

"I heard," Mr. Massey agreed.

"His assignment was a good idea. But," Rachel paused. "But you need to know something about me. If I decide on a word, that's it, I'm all in. The pressure to pick one word stuck with me all summer. I just couldn't find the right one. I'm prepared to take a zero on this assignment because I don't want to pick a word just to finish the homework. I want to find a word that really means something to me and I'm sorry I couldn't find one over the summer."

Mr. Massey smiled, which surprised Rachel.

"You're smiling?" Rachel asked.

Mr. Massey nodded. "I guess I am. Can I tell you a secret?" He leaned in close to her.

Rachel nodded.

"Mr. Smith is my good friend. I think he'd be honored to know that you're taking the time to think about his message." Mr. Massey thought for a moment and then snapped his fingers. "I've got an idea."

"I'm all ears," Rachel said, leaning in.

"I have a sign-up sheet for reading essays during this first week. Our newest student, who hasn't heard a thing about *My Special Word* yet, will go last. Why don't you take the spot right before him on Thursday afternoon?"

Rachel beamed.

"Even if you can't find a word by Thursday, you will still write an essay. It might be an essay about how hard it was for you to pick a word, but it will be an essay. Deal?"

Just as Mr. Massey finished talking, there was a knock on his classroom door.

Principal Imar led a boy into the room. "Mr. Massey, this is Xander, and Mr. and Mrs. Lucas." Two adults stepped into the room behind the boy. Rachel walked across the room and extended a hand to Xander.

"Hi," she said. "I'm Rachel. Welcome to Rubye Irene Elementary School."

Xander shook her hand. "Hey," he said. "Um, thanks."

"Rachel will be able to show you where to hang up your things and where your desk is," Mr. Massey said. Xander's parents smiled as Mr. Massey guided them around the classroom. He showed them the science tables in the back and the reading corner with beanbag chairs near the window.

"Rachel," Mr. Massey called from the reading corner. "Can you tell Xander a bit about *My Special Word* and help him get settled? Maybe you could show him the sign-up sheet, too. It's on my desk." Mr. Massey gave Rachel a thumbs up. She returned the move. She was happy to help Xander feel welcome.

"*My Special Word*?" Xander asked. "That sounds, uh, interesting?"

"Totally interesting, and awesome, and, uh, difficult," Rachel joked. Well, maybe it wasn't so much of a joke because it was hard to pick the right word.

Xander and Rachel walked to Mr. Massey's desk. She wrote her name in the next to last spot on the sign-up sheet. "You'll go here," she said, pointing to the last spot.

"Okay," Xander said. "What am I signing up for?"

"Last year, a special guest came to the school and told us about a program that he developed called *My Special Word*. He talked about how if you find a word that really means something to you, you can use that word to *live by*, a word that will help you be a better individual and make the world a better place.

My friend Nene picked the word *cool* because she stays cool under pressure. You'll meet Matthew soon, too. He picked *smart*."

"What word did you pick?" Xander asked.

"I didn't," Rachel said, without a hint of sadness in her voice.

"You didn't?" Xander asked and raised his eyebrows.

"Not yet. We were supposed to pick a word over the summer and *live by* that word, then write an essay about a time that the word guided us. But I got hung up on finding the perfect word and I couldn't do the assignment. Mr. Massey is giving me until Thursday to complete the assignment." Rachel held her hand near her mouth and whispered, "He seems really nice."

"Looks like he's giving me until Thursday, too," Xander said, pointing to the sign-up sheet.

"Yep," Rachel said.

Just then, Mr. Massey stepped up behind Rachel and Xander. "I'm going to walk Mr. and Mrs. Lucas out. Why don't you go watch Mr. Smith's video in the library? By the time you get back, the rest of the class will be here," Mr. Massey said.

"The video. That's right," Rachel said. "Great idea." Rachel remembered the video they watched last year on MySpecialWord.com that showed Mr. Smith talking about the program.

"One problem," Xander said. "Where's the library?"

Mr. Massey laughed. "I think your new friend can show you." Mr. Massey walked into the hallway, and Rachel and Xander followed. Xander waved goodbye to his mom and dad.

"This way," Rachel said, turning in the opposite direction.

"They're watching us walk away, aren't they?" Xander asked.

Rachel looked over her shoulder. "Yep," she said.

"Parents can be so weird," Xander said, then both he and Rachel cracked up laughing. "I don't know why you had such a hard time picking your word," Xander said. "It seems pretty obvious to me."

"Oh yeah?" Rachel said.

"Friend," Xander said. "You seem like a pretty good one so far."

Rachel smiled. "Thanks for the suggestion."

"No problem," Xander said. "I think I have my word, too."

"Oh yeah?" Rachel said again. "What is it?"

Xander shook his head. "Oh no. You'll have to wait until Thursday, just like everyone else."

"Fair enough," Rachel said. "I can hardly wait, my friend."

Chapter 8

BASKETBALL

Rachel stepped off the bus after an awesome first day of school. She couldn't wait to see her mom to tell her all about it. When Rachel got to the front door, she saw a note hanging near the knob.

"Meet me on the court. I have a super surprise for your first day of fifth grade. Love, Mom."

Rachel raced around the back of the townhouse to see her mom on the court. She had a red and white blanket spread out under the hoop.

"A picnic!" her mom called, waving Rachel over.

Rachel dropped her backpack in the grass and hurried over to meet her mom.

"All your favorites," her mom said. "Pickles, Doritos, and chicken salad on rye."

Rachel reached for the bag of Doritos first, a snack she rarely got to have but one that she loved. The orange of the cheese reminded her of the color of her favorite basketball.

"And to drink," Rachel's mom said, pulling two bottles out of the shopping bag at her side. "Chocolate milk."

Rachel grabbed for the bottle, too. This was the best surprise to top off an already awesome day.

"Tell me all about it," her mom said. So Rachel told her mom about talking with Mr. Massey in the morning, and meeting Xander, and how she and Nene sat together at lunch, and how she got to have gym class twice a week in fifth grade.

"Wow, sounds like the start to a great year," her mom said. "Now for the icing on the cake."

"There's cake, too?" Rachel asked, her eyes growing wide.

"Ha! Nope. But I do have this," her mom said, holding up a container of sidewalk chalk.

"Chalk? That's my cake?" Rachel frowned.

"I thought we could make a list of some words, in chalk, big and bold, right here on the basketball court."

Rachel nodded her head. "I'm in," she said. "On second thought, let's not do it right here. How about off to the side where it'll wash off?"

"That's what I meant," her mom said. "I would never trash your court!" Her mom took the bin of chalk across the sideline and wrote *respects property* at the top of the list.

"That's two words," Rachel said. She grabbed a piece of chalk and wrote *respectful*.

Rachel and her mom went back and forth adding words to the list. By the time they were finished, they had a string of words longer than Rachel, from her head to her toes.

"Let's do this," her mom said. She pulled a pink piece of chalk from the bin. "Cross off the ones that you aren't excited about. Don't think too hard."

Rachel's mom sighed as soon as Rachel crossed out *smart*. "I told you, Matthew picked smart."

She kept crossing off words until just one remained. *Basketball.*

"That's it!" her mom yelled and then jumped up and down. "Bas-ket-ball! Bas-ket-ball! Bas-ket-ball!" She cheered.

Rachel frowned. "I don't think that's what Mr. Smith had in mind, Mom. He wanted us to pick a word to *live by*, not something that we like to do."

Her mom circled the word anyway. "I get that. Promise me you'll take some time to think about how *basketball* might work. Deal?"

"Deal," Rachel said. She looked at the word again and then back up at her mom. "Now, how about that cake?"

Her mom laughed and shook her head. "Doritos and chocolate milk right under your nose and you want cake?"

Rachel got an idea. She ran across the yard and picked up a basketball that was on the ground. It was an old one that had probably been outside since last winter. She tried to dribble it on the way back to the court but it just plopped down on the ground.

"Needs some air," she said. "But I can still make something sweet with it."

Rachel locked her feet on the three-point line, took a pretend dribble with the dead ball, and sent it flying.

Swoosh!

Rachel gave a wave of her fingers at the hoop.

"Nice follow through," her mom said. "Dead ball and all."

"I can always make it work, even with a droopy ball," Rachel said.

"And you didn't even mess up the picnic," her mom said, picking up the ends of the picnic blanket.

Rachel helped her mom pack up the sweet surprise. She grabbed her backpack from the side of the court and stuffed the deflated ball under her arm. Rachel took one last look at the list of words on the side of the court before following her mom into the house. She wondered if *basketball* could work. What was it about the word that meant something to her? Was it just the sport? The ball? Or something more about the game of basketball?

Chapter 9

GOOD SPORT

Two days later, Rachel was still considering *basketball* as her word. She thought a lot about how much the sport meant to her. It was special to be a part of a team, and cool to learn from someone like Coach G.

It was important for her to stay focused during games and she liked that shooting hoops helped clear her mind. There was so much about the sport that she loved but she still wasn't quite sure how that made the word something she could *live by* the way Mr. Smith had said.

"Welcome to Wednesday," Mr. Massey said. "We've got six superheroes to hear from today with *My Special Word* essays and you've got gym and art class today. Double awesome. And we are learning about— drumroll, please— similes during language arts today! I'm as excited as a bumblebee at the Rose Bowl." Mr. Massey laughed. "See what I did there?"

Rachel got it and she laughed with Mr. Massey. Only a few days into fifth grade and she couldn't believe how lucky she was to have such a great teacher. Mr. Massey was kind and pretty funny. She also couldn't believe how lucky she was to have one more day to write her essay, thanks to Mr. Massey.

"How's it going?" Xander asked as the class lined up to walk to art.

"Good. You?"

"Good, but I mean, how's it going with your word?" Xander whispered.

Just then, Mr. Massey reminded the line to get quiet for the hallway.

Rachel gave Xander a thumbs up to let him know that things were going really well with her word.

By the end of the day, Rachel was almost positive that she knew her word. There was just one problem with the word. Rachel moved forward in her seat; she leaned close to Nene to ask one quick question.

"All right," Mr. Massey said. "Deeja is our last friend to read today. Please give her your attention."

"Nene," Rachel whispered. But at that moment, Deeja cleared her throat and started reading. Rachel sat back in her seat to listen. She could save her question for later.

"My word is not actually a word. It's two words." Deeja started. "Good sport."

Rachel sat up straight. That was her problem. Two words, not one. Then Rachel smiled. Good sport was a perfect word for her classmate. (Or perfect *words,* as Deeja put it.)

"I have six brothers," Deeja continued. "Six. Summertime means playing lots of games with them. Uno, checkers, soccer, tic-tac-toe. Especially when it's raining." Deeja pointed out the classroom window at the rain storm. "But I'm the oldest, so I think my job is to show my brothers how to be a *good sport.* That means being a good winner or a gracious loser.

I really thought about my word when my brother Martin lost at checkers one day and he threw the board. He threw it all the way across our kitchen. Baby Sami started crying.

I won, but it didn't feel that great because Martin was so upset. I went and talked to him about what it means to lose graciously. I talked to him about how when you lose you need to think about it as practice. Practice that might make him win in the future. He hugged me and asked if I would play with him again. I did. I won again.

But he didn't throw the board; instead he said, 'good game' like I taught him and shook my hand like I taught him. That made winning feel even better. We could both be good sports together even though one person won and one person lost."

Deeja took a little bow when she stopped reading. Mr. Massey started clapping and we all followed.

"Good sport. I like it," Mr. Massey said. "Go hang your essay up on the wall for me."

Rachel thought Deeja's essay was the best so far. She couldn't wait to share her word— well, *words*— with her class tomorrow.

"Just three friends left to read their essays," Mr. Massey said. "Then I have a surprise to share with all of you about *My Special Word*."

Another surprise?

Cedar Point.

Mr. Massey being so understanding.

A new friend.

The basketball court picnic.

And a *My Special Word* surprise.

Rachel wasn't sure how much better fifth grade could get, but after the first few days, she felt like this year was a slam-dunk. Everything was finally coming together thanks to Rachel's hard word and Deeja's *good sport*.

Chapter 10

WORD

Rachel got home from school and went straight to her bedroom. She pulled the paper with the *My Special Word* assignment on it in front of her. She wrote like her fingers were on fire. The words came pouring out. She filled the entire front of the page and had to flip it over to the back.

It felt great. The essay was finally finished and she had found the best words to *live by*.

"Knock, knock," her mom said before peeking into Rachel's room. "Good news; the sun is out."

"Better news," Rachel said holding up the paper. "My essay is finished."

Rachel's mom stepped into her room. "Can I read it?"

Rachel handed over the paper. She watched as her mom's eyes scanned the page, line by line. She flipped the page over and continued to read. When her eyes rested on the last word, she smiled.

"Oh, Rachel," her mom said. "It's perfect."

"Thanks, Mom," Rachel said. "I'm really proud of it."

Her mom handed the paper back to her. "Any other homework?"

Rachel shook her head.

"Well, why don't you spend some time at the hoop while I make dinner? Sun's out. Work's done. Looks like you've got time to shoot around."

Rachel grabbed her ball from the floor. The good one. No dead-end, deflated ball today. She was ready to spin, hop, dribble, and drive to the net.

She spent the next hour hitting shots from all over the court: free throws, lay-ups, and her favorite, sweet spot at the tip of the three-point curve.

"Nice follow through," her mom called after one of her free throws dropped straight into the net. Her mom jogged out onto the court. "Dinner is ready."

"You're right, Mom. I've always had a great follow through," Rachel said, then winked.

Her mom planted her hands on her hips and narrowed her eyes at Rachel. "You do have good follow through now, but you didn't always. You worked hard to make it good."

Her mom was right. Rachel had to work hard and practice a lot to perfect her follow through, both on and off the court. She looped her arm into her mom's and they started back to their house.

The storm from earlier had washed away most of the chalked words from Rachel's list, except one. The word *basketball* remained, even the dark pink circle her mom had drawn around it. Rachel smiled as they passed the word on their way back inside for dinner. She liked that *basketball* remained because without it she would never have found her special word.

The next morning, Rachel flew out of bed. She got dressed lickety-split, packed her paper carefully, and then rushed out to the basketball court. When her mom heard the familiar sound of dribbling behind the house, she went outside, too.

"Want a ride?" her mom called.

Rachel didn't let the question break her concentration; instead, she lined her elbow up with the rim and sent her basketball through the air. Once it dropped into the net, Rachel turned her attention to her mom.

"Thanks, but I'll take the bus."

"Okay," her mom said, nodding. "You all set for today?"

"You know it," Rachel said.

"That's what I like to hear," her mom said. "Two more shots, then come in for breakfast before the bus gets here."

Rachel took her shots, then ran home for breakfast. She could hardly keep her milk inside her cereal bowl; she was so excited to finally share her word at school.

The bus ride seemed longer than usual as she waited to pull up outside her school. Her legs jumpy-jittery bounced the whole ride.

When Rachel stepped from the bus, Nene called, "Hey, Rachel."

"Hey, Nene." Rachel caught up to her friend near the school's entrance.

"Feeling good?" Nene asked. "Because you look like you're feeling good."

Rachel blushed. "I can't wait to share my word today," she said. "Do you really think Mr. Massey will make me wait until the end of the day like he has for everyone else?"

Nene held the door open for her friend. "I do. I also believe he will have some cheesy joke to start our day."

"Cheesy?" Rachel asked. "You mean hilarious!"

Nene and Rachel laughed all the way to Mr. Massey's classroom.

"Well isn't that just the best way to start your day?" Mr. Massey asked as the girls giggled their way into the room. Suddenly, Mr. Massey's face turned serious. "Rachel, can I see you at my desk?" he said.

Rachel pulled her homework folder from her backpack and quickly hung up her bag before meeting Mr. Massey at his desk.

"I just wanted to check in with you," Mr. Massey said, pointing to the sign-up sheet on his desk. "You'll follow Jackson this afternoon with your essay, right?"

"Yes," Rachel said. "Why wait? I can share it first thing this morning!"

"Glad to hear it, but I think we'll stick with the plan. I'm a man with a plan," he said.

Mr. Massey got the class settled and went over the day's schedule. Rachel's leg bobbed underneath her desk the whole time.

Xander leaned across the aisle towards her. "Nervous?" he whispered.

Rachel shook her head. "I'm pumped," she whispered back.

Xander smiled. Rachel had a feeling he was pumped, too. She sailed through gym and lunch, a new story in reading class, and a few more jokes from Mr. Massey. Before Rachel knew it, the end of the day had arrived.

"All right," Mr. Massey said. "Just three final essays from three fine friends." Mr. Massey pointed to Jackson, then Rachel, and finally Xander, as he said, "One, two, and three."

"And then you'll tell us the surprise?" Matthew said from his seat at the front of the room.

"Yes, Matthew. Then I will tell you all the super, awesome, fan-tab-u-louso *My Special Word* surprise. But first, please give it up for my friend, Jackson Bishop." The class erupted in applause for Jackson who reluctantly slid from his desk to stand at the front of the room.

He cleared his throat a few times. Rachel could tell he was anxious. She guessed that Mr. Massey could tell, too, because he said, "Jackson, you've got this. Just tell us your word."

"My word is *turtle*," Jackson said.

Everyone laughed. Jackson's face turned bright red.

"Whoa, whoa, whoa," Mr. Massey said. "This is the most interesting word I've heard all day," he continued. "Settle down so we can hear why Jackson picked *turtle*."

Mr. Massey went and stood next to Jackson. Rachel noticed the way Jackson's shoulders relaxed with Mr. Massey by his side.

"I picked the word *turtle* for a few reasons. One, I got a *turtle* this summer. A red-eared slider. He's not a baby; he is ten, like me. His name is Turtonater. He's quiet and kind of shy, like me. Another reason I picked *turtle* is because turtles like to do the same thing every day, over and over." Jackson paused and looked up at Mr. Massey. "Like you, turtles like to know the plan. Me too. And," Jackson went on. "Turtles are pretty brave when they have to be. Like, to get back to their home, they might cross a busy road. We saw a turtle do that on the road near my grandma's house this summer. I can be brave if I have to be." Jackson looked up at Mr. Massey again. "I don't want to say this last part."

"Want me to read it?" Mr. Massey asked.

Jackson shook his head.

"Okay," Mr. Massey said. "Thank you for sharing your word with us, Jackson. Please hang your essay up on the board over there." Mr. Massey pointed to the wall where all of the other essays hung.

Rachel knew it was just about her time but she waited for Jackson to finish hanging his essay. She understood what a big deal it was for Jackson to stand up in front of the class and read.

She wondered if the last part of his essay had something to do with hiding in a shell because she thought Jackson might want to do just that most days. She would remember to read the last part of his essay and tell him how brave she thought he was for getting up in front of the class.

"We're ready for you, Rachel," Mr. Massey said. He waved his arm towards the front of the room like he was inviting her onto a stage. Rachel wasn't afraid to be in the spotlight. It was like being on the free throw line, with all eyes watching her take a shot. She just had to focus.

"Good luck," Nene whispered as Rachel passed by her desk.

Rachel stood at the front of the room. She smiled at Nene and then at Mr. Massey before she began. "Just like Deeja, my special word is actually two words: *follow through*. I thought all summer about what my word could be and I almost dropped the ball on this assignment, but I didn't because I have *follow through*. I play a lot of basketball and Coach G and my mom are always telling me that I have nice *follow through* on my shots. I know what that means on the court."

Rachel set her paper down on Mr. Massey's desk and pretended to shoot a basketball. "See the way my hand hangs here?" Rachel wiggled her fingers. "See the way my wrist turns down like I'm reaching into a cookie jar on a high shelf?"

A few kids giggled, Rachel knew that they weren't laughing at her, just the move she described. She grabbed her paper from Mr. Massey's desk and kept reading. "That's what *follow through* looks like when I'm shooting a ball but *follow through* without a basketball is just as important to me. *Follow through* means sticking with something even when it is tough, like this assignment.

It's showing up and doing what you are supposed to do. Or being where you are supposed to be, especially when someone else is counting on you." Rachel looked right at Nene before continuing.

"There are times that my *follow through* is really good: on the court, this assignment, but there were times this summer that I didn't have great *follow through* and that is something I want to be better at. I missed my best friend's birthday party and that wasn't good *follow through*. She counted on me being there and I let her down. But what I think Mr. Smith wanted was for us to try to *live by* our words, and not just in the summer, but always.

I think that means that I get to try my best to *follow through* on being a better friend going forward. That is why I picked the words *follow through* to *live by*."

Rachel looked up from her paper to a sea of smiling faces, Nene's was the biggest and brightest.

"Well done, Rachel," Mr. Massey said. "Before you hang up your essay, let me see something." Mr. Massey slipped Rachel's essay paper from her hands. His eyes scanned the page. "Right here, 'I think Mr. Smith wanted was for us to try to *live by* our words, and not just in the summer, but always.' Did you guys hear that line in Rachel's essay?"

Rachel's classmates nodded while Mr. Massey handed the page back to Rachel.

"Well, that is one huge clue towards the surprise we have with *My Special Word.*" Mr. Massey held up his hand like a stop sign. "But, you'll have to wait until Mr. Xander shares his word before I tell you the rest," he said.

The boys and girls whispered ideas about the surprise while Rachel hung up her essay on the wall. She took an extra moment to straighten the page so it would hang just right. That seemed like good *follow through* to her.

On her way back to her seat, she saw Xander coming towards her. He took a deep breath and raised his hand to meet hers as they passed. When their hands met in a high five, Rachel felt like she was spreading some lucky vibes to her new friend. That seemed like good *follow through* too.

Rachel was ready to live her word every day. She knew that some days might be hard, but she hoped that she would remember on those tough days just how good it felt to do the right thing, like finishing the assignment.

She also knew that the more she practiced, the stronger she would be. Just like out on the court, she would *follow through* with her special word.

www.myspecialword.com

My Special Word continues…

Book 2: Discover Xander's word in ***Xander Bounces Back*** out September 2017.

Alison Green Myers

is a writer.

Her word is **GOODWILL**.

GOODWILL means caring about the health and happiness of others. She strives to be an activist of goodwill.

*

Dwight Smith

is the co-founder of My Special Word.

His word is **SOLD**.

He is **SOLD** on his faith. He uses this word to help him make humble, helpful choices in his life.

What's your word?

Share it with us at **www.myspecialword.com**.